Spartan + FRIENDS
I0746539

Pypah's Pony

Colouring and Literacy Book

Consolidating phonics knowledge with extended decodable text.

Word Count

Approx. 283 words

Focus Phonics Sounds

ow – cows
ai – rain
ee – cheer
sh – she'd
th – with
ch – charm

High-Frequency Words

the, and, a, to, in, was, said, she, her, they, went, had, with, for, as, out, it, on, of, by

Irregular Words

said, was, you, your, they, their, were, because, friend, through

Practice Words

Pypah, Suki, Remi, pony, saddle, bridle, trot, canter, ride, horse, farm, lesson, brush, creek, field, trust, proud, smile, brave

Teacher Prep Before Reading

Phonics Warm-Up: Review ee, ai, and ow sounds (cheer, rain, cows) using flashcards

Vocabulary Support: Introduce or discuss – ony, saddle, bridle, trot, canter, trust, courage, friendship.

Prediction Prompt: Ask: "How do you think Pypah will help Suki learn to trust her?"

Pypah beamed with happy cheer,
a pony gift was drawing near.
Her cousin Remi grinned and said,
"Suki's yours to love instead!"

Suki had been out with the cows,
chewing grass beneath the trees.
She'd flick her tail and trot away,
She liked her space most every day.

It took some time, she'd run and dart,
unsure of trust, a nervous start.
At last she came with steady charm,
and off they went to Aunt Kirsty's farm.

Her coat was dappled, soft and grey,
her mane like clouds on a windy day.
Pypah whispered, calm and slow,
"It's okay, Suki, we will take it slow."

She brought some hay and stayed a while,
talking softly with a smile.
Suki sniffed, then took a bite,
her ears turned forward, things felt right.

Each day she'd sit and hum a tune,
morning sun or late afternoon.
Step by step their trust grew true,
friendship sparkled, bright and new.

In the round yard, slow they'd go,
Pypah whispered soft and low.
Step and stop, then start once more,
their hearts in rhythm, trust would soar.

**Aunty Kirsty showed her how,
to brush and saddle Suki now.
The saddle was snug, the girth pulled tight,
Pypah beamed, it felt just right!**

The first ride made her tummy flip,
she gave the reins a careful grip.
They trotted slow, she sat up tall,
and Aunt Kirsty's cheer was best of all!

**The next week Pypah started lessons,
learning with Tayah by her side.
"Steer and stop and turn with care,
show kind hands and ride with pride."**

Rain or shine they'd practice still,
cantering past the gum-tree on the hill.
Each ride brought joy and balance too,
her confidence and courage grew.

“I’ll ride with you!” said Aunty Kirsty,
“Dot and Spartan too, what do you say?”
Pypah grinned from cheek to cheek,
her dream ride planned for next week!

The saddles gleamed, the bridles tight,
they set off laughing, it was pure delight.
Suki's hooves went clip-clop-clip,
through bush, creek and along the gumtree strip.

Aunty Kirsty rode Dot that day,
her mane was bright and gold,
Bec on Spartan trotted near,
so strong and brave and bold.
Pypah's smile lit up the sky,
as black cockatoos flew on by.

They rode through ferns and flowers smelling sweet,
where bees and pollen softly meet.
Suki pranced with head held high.
"I trust you, Pypah to be my guide!"

Now every week they ride with pride,
through open fields and across the countryside.
From wobbly steps to a steady flow,
their bond shines bright wherever they go.

Activities (for after reading)

1. Re-read the story and circle words with ai sound (trail)

2. Find and underline all the words with ee sound (trees)

3. Write 3 new sentences that include ar sounds (farm)

____

____

____

____

____

____

____

____

4. Pretend to be Suki and act out how she might move.

5. Fill the gap: Pypah whispered, __________ and slow

Activities (for after reading)

6.Write a short story about where you would want to ride your pony if you were Pypah. Make sure you include all the things you might see along the ride.

Activities (for after reading)

7. Write some words that rhyme with "bee."

____

____

8. Can you name some things Pypah did to gain Suki's trust?

____

____

____

9. What do you think was the most exciting part for Pypah, being gifted Suki, or going on the trail ride? Why?

____

____

____

____

____

Activities (for after reading)

10. Can you retell the important parts of the story?

____

____

11. What was your favourite part of story?

____

____

____

12. Draw what Suki might be thinking in a thought bubble during their first lesson.

Activities (for after reading)

13. Draw a line back to the phonics sound that matches the word

ee sound **sh sound**

trees showed

brush gumtree

bee creek

14. Complete the words with the missing sounds:

tr__s
s__n
cr__k
sw__t
br___t

15. Colour in all of the story pages.

What you will need:
Paper Plate, Cardstock, Black Felt Pen
Joggle Eye, Glue and Paint.

How to make it:
Paint the Backside of a paper plate the colour you would like your pony to be.

Trace the pattern provided on the next page onto tracing paper. (Backing Paper works well.) Transfer onto cardstock and cut out the shapes for the mane, ears and muzzle.

Assemble and glue the pieces onto the paper plate.

Glue on the joggle eyes. (You could also draw these on if you dont have any joggle eyes.)

Use the felt pen to draw on the nose and mouth features.

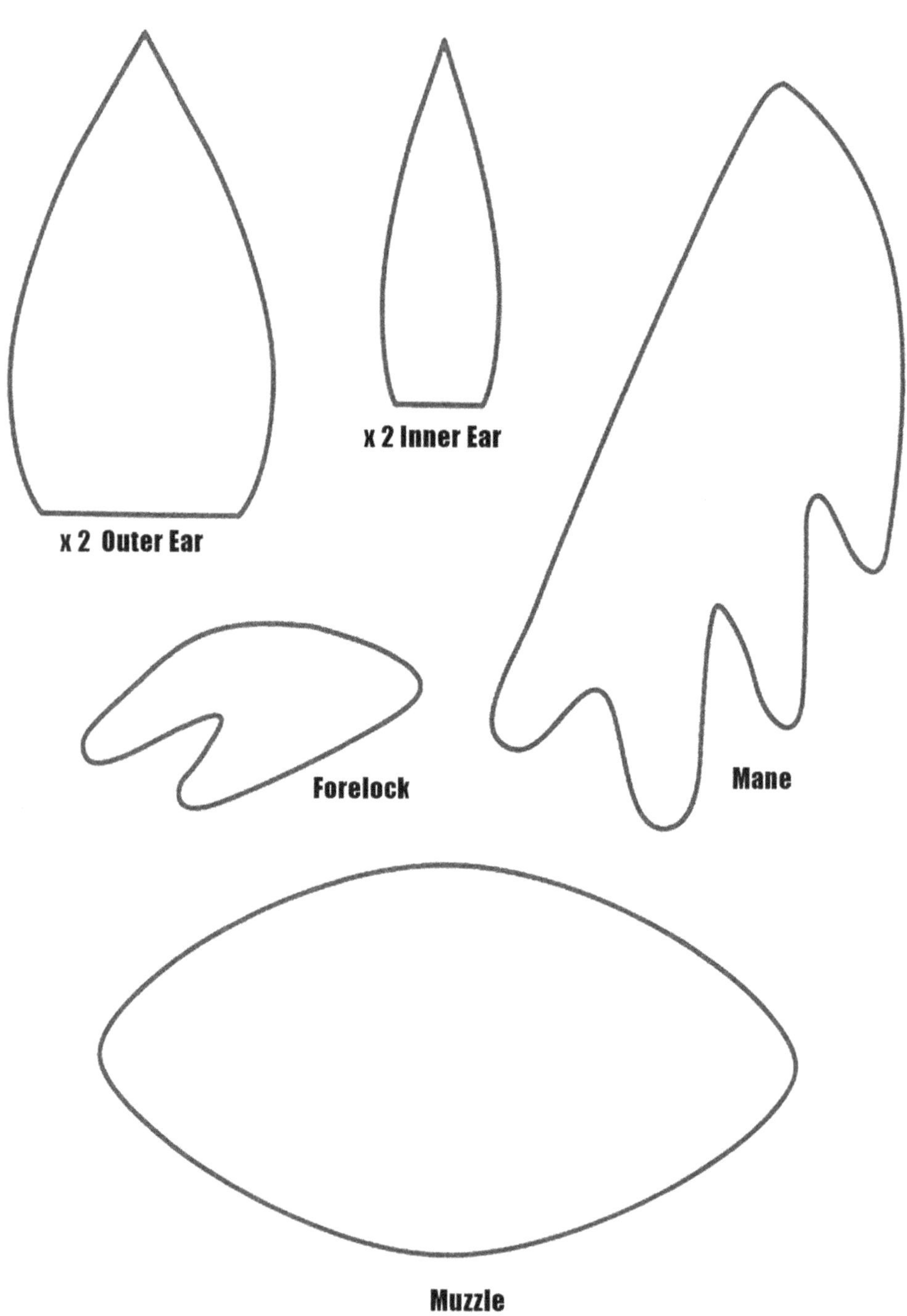

Paper Plate Pony Pattern

Spartan +
FRIENDS

www.ingramcontent.com/pod-product-compliance
Lightning Source LLC
Chambersburg PA
CBHW040548170726
48295CB00012B/629

9781764367400